A Creative Collection

of Short Stories & Poetry

Suzanne Strong

GREEN ACRE
PUBLISHING

ISBN: 9780648673262
Green Acre Publishing

DEDICATION

For Leah and Micah.

CONTENTS

DANCING SHOES

Dancing Shoes

Edges crumpled in triangles on two corners of a fading poster, plastered onto the door of the Rio Rhythmic Dance Studio. Proud vivid feathers stand at attention to the sky, mingling with shimmering sequined head dresses on bronze kissed women's heads, winking glittering bra tops, barely concealing nipples, exposed skin, silver navel ornaments falling to tasseled tenuous briefs. Arms outstretched, hips moving like some other force was in control like the women were as artificial as they appeared, warming themselves in the adoration of men, "Stepford Wives," breathtakingly beautiful and robotic male creations.

Genève and I both saw it and looked at each other and laughed. The same question on each other's faces, what were we doing here? A Latin beat and melody drifted down the corridor getting louder as we climbed the stairs. Reaching the top we saw Juan the dance Instructor, who smiled at us from across the room.

"Hello ladies. Come in make yourselves at home," he said in a dense Latin American seesawing accent.

His body was like a muscular figurine, dark and well defined; through his brief singlet top most of his taut, hairless chest could be seen. His tight, black pants revealed a pert spherical bottom. He was the cliché of a Latin Lover/Dancer. Walking over to his side of the room. He smiled at us, looking us up and down, what else would you expect?

"We'll make Latin dancers out of you girls, if it kills us."

"It may do so too," Gen said laughing. I glanced at Gen, grateful she was there with me, as she always was.

Around the room people were stretching, some were staring awkwardly into the middle, a middle aged couple looked like they were trying to rekindle their love instead they regarded each other awkwardly, a single mother and daughter in school uniform also stood uncomfortably looking at Juan. There were the two pulling up leg warmers, in tights and long t-shirts, their hair frizzed up and pulled back by white bandanas (what was this was an episode from Flash Dance or something? And it was a sizzling hot Brisbane summer, after all!)

Another middle-aged couple stood as if they were about to go on stage for a professional performance – their bodies held in the rumba position ready to launch into a routine. You just wanted to walk up behind them and say, "hey, lighten up."

"This is a beginners class isn't it?" I asked Gen.

"Supposed to be," she said, also looking at the couple.

Juan called everyone's attention.

"Hello everyone, welcome," said Juan, his white smile passed over everyone like a midnight beacon over the dark surging ocean.

A guy who would've been mid-thirties with dark curly hair, vibrant blue eyes with lines around them that reflected kindness and a delicate smile like a swallow, whispered to his blonde friend who was wearing board shorts, a t-shirt and no shoes. They looked how I felt; out of place.

"We'll start with the basic moves and then later we'll get you to dance with partners."

A drumbeat reverberated, percussion began to frenzy and the charango drove the rhythm of the music as Juan clapped his hands and moved his hips in circular motion, clicking his tongue and saying, "let's get moving."

"Whoa, I hope he doesn't expect us to do that," I whispered to Gen watching his gyrations and referring to his clicking abandonment. She laughed quietly. His body was a robot as his hips traced circles in the air, whilst his upper torso remained static.

"This is what we do in Latin Dance, the basis for all of our dances, this hip movement. Aussies find this hard to do," he said, moving his hips from side to side in perfect formation.

"Move your hips, not your upper body..." We began moving and Juan walked around us and touched some of our hips, male and female moving them in the right direction. Then he got us walking around in a circle, whilst moving our hips. Most of us were struggling, the experienced couple were moving with precision. Genève and I looked at each other and laughed.

"Australians are so uptight they do not move their hips much, we Brazilians do it all the time," Juan said, laughing.

After multiple circles around the studio and watching ourselves in the mirror, Juan allowed us to break. Some of the people were breathless and going various shades of light maroon. One lady was sweating and breathless so much she could've been a candidate for a heart attack.

Gen and I retrieved our water bottles, chatting about how we were finding it when I suddenly became aware of someone walking towards us. I turned to see the dark man with his blonde friend. Uh oh, I hated these awkward conversations, particularly with men. I was so out of practice.

The dark haired man introduced himself as Mark looked directly at me, his smile lighting up his features and the man with straw-coloured hair was David.I introduced us and leant against the mirror behind me.

"You guys done this before?" David asked.

"Nope, can't you tell?" I said.

"You've been fine," Mark answered.

"Gen's got it down pat. It is going to take me longer because I haven't danced since high school."

"Not really."

Juan began clapping his hands and started calling out to the group.

"Now is time for partner dance."

Juan came towards us and paired up Mark and I and Gen and David together. Then he continued on pushing together people in an authoritarian voice. We were told to stand in close proximity to one another, lacing our fingers together in a coat hanger like shape.

This stance I hadn't been in since my wedding waltz, which should be more aptly termed a wedding sway. And look how that had turned out. Six months since my marriage break up, but I still felt sick and adrenalin pulsed through my legs. It felt as if I was somehow betraying someone.

Mark and I faced each other. Awkwardness directed Mark's limbs as he shifted his weight and his eyes dropped every now and then. I avoided looking directly into Mark's eyes that were both gentle and alluring, but seemed confronting to me. It was a strange feeling being close to another man other than Steve, and now, feeling jittery around someone. Then his words collided around my mind; "fuckin' bitch," "slut" and I felt his hands around my neck...I hadn't thought about Steve for a while but every now and then these scenes played as a short film before me. Breathing in I returned to the here and now. Mark looked at me in an inquisitive manner, questions clouding his face. Looking down at my shoes, I sought to hide my emotions. My gaze turned to the middle aged married couple next to us and I smiled. They smiled back, then turned and glared at each other.

"You okay? It's not going to be that bad dancing with me," Mark said with a crooked cheeky smile.

"Of course," I said laughing, "I'm a bit nervous about how I will be as a dancing partner."

"You'll be fine." he said squeezing my hand.

"Pull your partner a little closer," Juan called.

Mark's warm hand rested on the curve of my lower back, he pulled me close and tightened the embrace. Adrenalin filled my limbs, how ridiculous I thought. Less air separated us now, our bodies close, I looked at the contours of his neck bones, his hands were large and somewhat cold from sweat, his warmth touched my chest. Goose bumps rose tiny round mountains on my skin. His cologne surrounded me, strong and delicious like fresh wood shavings on a carpentry floor. His breath touched my neck and I wanted to relax into it. He looked into my eyes. I looked away. Faint lines around the edge of his lips formed a kind smile.

"No really, are you okay?"

"Yep, sorry about that. I'm elsewhere."

Juan called out commands and we sought to follow. Mark was better than I thought and we moved well together. I focused on the steps, the movement of my legs and feet in unison with his and the movement of my hips under his large hands. Shifting my attention from Mark, I honed in on Juan's words to everyone.

Mark and I stumbled. Juan came over and corrected our positioning and movements. He positioned our bodies closer together, we started the Samba, which involved steps forward and backward and was elegant. Then we moved onto the Rumba, which included a circular gyration of our pelvises and hips together reminiscent of certain other human actions. Now that was not a little awkward, I was already nervous enough.

Alternating turns and being spun out from Mark and around, movements of our hips in sensuous unison, our cohesion didn't always work but was extremely humourous. We couldn't stop laughing but sought to maintain composure when Juan looked over. Sweet strumming of guitars flamenco style, individual high-pitched plucked notes and honey harmonic male voices serenaded our steps. Juan kept telling me to look into Mark's eyes. So I did. Over the 45 minutes my inhibitions dissipated. Gen and David were next to us, we all chatted and laughed as we sought to emulate the dance, but mostly made mistakes

When Juan said "that is it for couple work tonight," I was disappointed.

"Thanks, everyone. Give yourselves a clap, you did very well."

I clapped sheepishly, glancing at Mark, chuckling as our stumbles replayed in my mind. He smirked back.

"Thanks Sade, you were a great partner."

"Except for the bruises on your feet."

"Yeah, except for that." He winked at me and I smiled feeling self-conscious in a good way.

"How did you guys go?" Gen asked us, "Looked like you had heaps of fun."

"I did," I said.

"Me too," Mark agreed.

David and Mark said they'd see us next week. Mark turned briefly and caught my eyes, then disappeared. Gen looked at me turning her head to the side and said in a singing voice.

"He looked nice."

"Yeah he was."

I drank from my bottle, trying to seem nonchalant.

"Looked like he liked you."

"Don't think so. Even if he did, watch him run when he finds out about my life."

"You're so cynical."

"Not cynical, just realistic."

"Uh huh," Gen rolled her eyes.

I pulled her into a hug.

"You're a great friend to me," I said remembering the night I turned up at Gen's house distraught and with my children, after I left. She embraced me and took me in.

We walked towards the stairs and said our goodbyes to Juan. Descending the stairs we returned to our lives again. Gen to her husband and three children and me to my children and my veterinarian practice not far from here. The following week moved quickly; school drop offs, my daughter's soccer training, my son's art classes, my violin lessons, working and on the weekend brunch with Gen and Simone, while Steve had the kids for the day. I hadn't let him have them overnight, didn't know if I could trust him. He had taken them to the museum this time.

**

Stretching on the dance floor again, my senses became heightened as I noticed Mark across the room but no David. Someone was standing behind Mark. Then she appeared, tall, dark haired and wearing black pants and a fitted yellow singlet. She was leaning in close to Mark, chatting and laughing.

Typical. Of course, he wasn't single. He smiled and waved. I waved back and turned towards the mirror not knowing where to look.

"Looks like we'll have to get new partners, David's not here and Mark has a new partner," I said nudging Gen.

"Yep, looks like it. Attractive, isn't she?"

"Yeah," I said wondering why she had to rub it in.

Juan approached and paired us up with two guys standing nearby, looking lost on their first class. Peter, my partner, had ginger blonde hair, white skin with yellow tinges on the edges of his face and garlic emanated from every pore. Dancing with Peter was like slowly receiving dental treatment with no anaesthetic. Juan intervened on many occasions to no avail. After an eternity, Juan called a break, winking at me. I walked over to Gen.

"Scott would be jealous of what I saw you guys doing," I said patting her on the shoulder. A hand touched my arm. Uh oh, not Peter. Turning around I saw Mark's smiling face and his partner standing next to him.

"Hey."

"Hello, how are you?" I asked.

"Great thanks. Hey, this is my sister Therese."

"Hello," I said feeling relieved and addressing her directly, "you guys danced well together. The talent must run in the family."

They both laughed.

"Yeah we'll probably dance with different partners next week. Was just helping Tess get used to the class."

"Such a nice brother. Though you looked like you knew what you were doing."

"I have done a little before," she said surprisingly shy for someone so striking.

Mark explained David had the flu and Gen said to pass on our regards. Suddenly, Juan clapped his hands again. I sighed. Not back to Peter again. Mark put his hand on my arm again and said quietly, "hey do you want to have a coffee with me sometime?"

"Sure," I said managing a shy smile.

"What about Friday at Café Tempo, 10:30?"

"Sounds good."

"Here's my card if there are any problems."

I looked at it – he was an Environmental Engineer for the Queensland Government State Development department.

"Okay, cool thanks. Better get back to my partner you know."

Returning to Peter, an involuntary smile formed on my face throughout his pushing and shoving with me around the dance floor. Juan hovered close to us. He saw it was a lost cause.

"I'll match you with different dancers next week to compliment your skill level." He said and smiled knowingly at me when Peter had turned his back. I suppressed a giggle. My feet ached and I was pleased when Juan said class was over for the evening. Mark and his sister left pretty quickly, waving as they went.

"See you Friday," Mark called.

"Sure," I said.

"Ohhh, a date?" Gen asked when he had disappeared.

"We're having a coffee."

"Really? Hmmm, well let me know what happens, ok?" she said, raising her eyebrows and the tone of her voice.

"Will do."

**

Wandering along Vulture Street I looked into Avid Reader bookshop as I passed, trying not to look ahead to Café Tempo. Then I saw him; sitting outside, his dark abundance of hair framed his face and his eyes focused on the newspaper below him. As I got closer he looked up and smiled. We greeted each other with a kiss on the cheek. I sat down at the table and a friendly waiter with blonde straight hair took my order and left. All I could think was Mark only likes who he thinks I am.

"How've you been since Tuesday?"

"Good thanks, Mark."

"Good to hear," Mark said smiling at me in a contented manner, sipping his flat white from the edge of the white china cup.

"There's something you need to know Mark."

"That sounds ominous."

"It is a bit."

"Okay, spit it out- all ears." He turned his face directly towards me.

"I have two children and um…left an abusive marriage some months ago." I looked into my coffee cup. I hated pity or people knowing my business, but I had to be honest.

"Oh. I'm so sorry to hear that. Are you okay now?" His tone of voice quietened and held a tender inflection. He put his hand on my wrist and looked into my face.

"Thanks, Mark. I'm going well now. It's much easier than it was at first. I'm happier, stronger now."

"Must've been horrible. How are your kids taking everything?"

"Yeah, pretty well I think. I let them see him every second weekend in the day. They have told me they feel happier now than before."

A cool change fell over our coffee date like a brooding grey sky and southerly breeze. A characteristic Brisbane storm brewing on the horizon had rolled in and now started to pour with rain. I couldn't gauge his thoughts.

"Mark, if you're uncomfortable with this, it's cool. I know it's a lot to adjust to, before you just thought I was a single woman."

"Yeah, it is a lot."

"I don't expect anything, I just like you…" I felt vulnerable.

"I like you too," he said, "you know that."

"I realise things are more complicated than us liking each other. It's not like when we were young hey? Sometimes I wish it was. I was hoping we could still get to know each other, but I totally understand, whatever you want."

"I'm not sure what I think, Sade. I'd be happy to get to know each other and see what happens."

"Sounds good to me."

Mark finished drinking his flat white. He asked me about my kids, what they liked to do, where they went to school, what they were like. I answered him, all the while noticing his difference. Not cold, but changed. Who could blame him? It was a lot to absorb. After a little while, he said he had to go.

"Okay, see you then," I said.

I watched him walk away. He had my business card and we agreed we would see other at dancing. We'd see after that. The day was moving on, its hot breath becoming more stifling. Who knew what would happen? All I knew was I wouldn't spend a lot of time dwelling on it. I was free now.

I looked at the photo of my kids on my mobile phone. Closing my eyes I saw endless blue surrounding me.

A VOID DANCE

A Void Dance

Drunk on the adulation of the humming crowd beyond the blinding white, and the tequila shot he had downed, he staggered, then leaned into his characteristic seductive sway, exaggerating each step. "Wish you, wish you were mine…" His voice was deep and textured and his mouth touched the microphone intimately; his breath was loud and heavy as he examined the faces of the thousands of hungry people before him. A void, an emptiness was present in this stadium, masses of humanity, seething and moving, arms up, around and reaching out to touch him in some way. Their need as great as his; it was an unspoken exchange between them, a brief affair, a salacious "one night stand."

Thousands of women and men's faces, adoring, some crumbling under their emotion, ravenous for his gaze or acknowledgement even if for a second, like lions pacing waiting for their sinewy carcass at the zoo, a tinge of desperation mingled with violent objectification. The exchange was mutual.

He fixed his gaze on one tall blonde woman; her slender arms and fine shoulders excited him, her eyes looked back at him unflinching, strong and seductive. He wondered if they would meet later. Inside he felt this familiar falling feeling, like in his dreams very often, this sinking sensation in his gut he used to have when hurling himself off a cliff into the river of Ku-ring-gai National

Park. Though that had been exhilarating, this however, was not. It was more like an ache, an abyss, an anxiety and an imperceptible void. It was usually only momentary.

Until he turned his back on the crowd and faced his band, catching the eye of Tim who was beating his skins with characteristic ease and flair, like he was himself dancing on top of each of them. He shot Dylan a satisfied grin. The song climaxed and they strummed the last remaining chords. Silence only for a moment, then the band resumed the next song, the drums lead and Jai came in with deep, driving bass. The crowd roared, thousands of people he would never know.

On this expanse of wood, with lighting, erected amplifiers, electric guitars and bass, a mass of drums, lights and images streamed across the audience, he felt he could exist here forever. His body was robotic in its sensuality. His missed his long dark hair that used to cover his eyes, now he ran his fingers over the shiny wetness of his bald head. He was neither conscious of his body nor acting deliberately, as if he left his body when he performed, occupying a space above himself hovering over the circus below and perceiving himself from the outside.

His father used to line up all of his children and demand one by one they stated what they had achieved that week, made to justify their worth. Dylan remembered his father's closed fist slamming into his face; full and hard like a plank of wood that reverberated sheer pain through his sinuses and nasal cavities. These memories were fierce but it was his father's words that haunted him more; *no one will ever want you, look at you.* Dylan knew his wife, Sophie, loved him and Zac and Angel…but there were the women…always an insatiable desire for this. Sophie understood mostly; he always made sure she knew that he loved her and never would leave, but you know, he was who he was. "Dylan Johnson." Flashes of their more vehement fights recently, unsettled him now, but he reassured himself of her loyalty and love.

Sweet guitar chords, deep bass and the driving of the drums reverberated around him as a tangible landscape and delivered him away. As the song faded Dylan turned to Jai, Tim and Michael who all stood next to him now and they all linked hands and bowed.

His ears rang as he walked off stage. Even though he had worn earplugs, it never seemed to totally block out the wall of sound that remained. Back stage there was an ecstatic vibe, people sipping champagne, chatting with band members, leaning against the wall, women playing with long strands of their dyed red hair as they focused on every word that Jai, Tim and Michael were saying and laughed in shrill tones. Dylan laughed. "Ahhh boys," he thought. Images of those three from the past, flashed brief footage across his mind, everything they had been through, the births of both his children, Michael's recovery from drug addiction and subsequent divorce and the death of Jai's sister.

"Great show," he patted Jai and Tim on the shoulder as he passed.

"Fuck, yeah," Jai embraced Dylan in a magnanimous hug.

"As always," Tim answered with a cheeky expression.

Dylan smiled at both of them, that expansive, enigmatic grin curling at its edges that had appeared on many magazine covers, newspaper articles, online and television talk shows.

Their manager David tapped Dylan on the back.

"Hey man, Sophie gave me this to give to you."

"Weird, thanks mate."

"No worries. Pretty old school, old school love," David said chuckling.

Hearing her name shot a painful sensation through him that he couldn't explain. The sight of her handwriting on the envelope unnerved him, he didn't know why. Smiling briefly at a brunette and blonde on the way, Dylan went to his dressing room. He could party soon. Sitting down before his mirror, he poured himself a scotch and opened Sophie's letter. He sipped the scotch relieved there was a momentary break from everything. Opening it, he heard her voice as he read:

Hi Luke,

I can't do this anymore. You treat me like shit, your behaviour with women after shows is disgusting and you tell me I should be ok with it, your drinking, the pills, parties, your mood swings, irritability and rage. I'm exhausted in every way. You treat the kids badly and you're competitive with them, especially Zac. I thought I could handle the women and sometimes I hoped you would change, but clearly you don't want to. You always say you can't do "normal." What you mean is you want to do whatever you want, and fuck what I need. When you say you love me, it passes right through me as if I'm a ghost. You don't seem to know what love is. None of this fame shit is real, Luke. It used to be just us facing everything. When we met years ago, you chased me, wanted to prove your worth to me, doing things to please me, telling me you'd make it "I'll be someone, Sophe." I never understood this. I loved you already, Luke Johnson, quiet, shy and gentle. You were always Luke to me. Now I don't seem to know you at all. You're not the man I loved 10 years ago. I miss him. Was this ever you? I don't even know. I've been so alone for years now You act as if I'm lucky to be with you. You're so arrogant. Your personality changes - Dr Jekyll and Mr Hyde at times and it scares me when you yell and throw things. It's the same look you get when you see a new woman you want to chase. I don't want Zac to think this is how he should be or Angel to put up with this. You really don't care about me or anyone else, especially your kids. Whenever I raised your behaviour and tried to leave in the past, you'd argue yell and blame me. I have to leave, for myself and the kids. Don't try to find us. It's best we don't see each other for a while. I'll ring you so you can talk to the kids. Sophie.

Dylan threw his glass smashing it completely on the wall; golden brown liquid drew crooked lines down its whiteness. Tim and Jai appeared at the door. Dylan covered his face with his hands.

"What the fuck, Dylan?" Jai said.

Dylan didn't raise his head. After a pause he said, "she's left."

"What? That can't be true, she's left before man, don't worry she'll come back again," Jai said putting his hand on Dylan's shoulder.

"Sorry, man." Tim said.

Dylan didn't say anything and picked up his phone. Dialing Sophie's number he knew it would go straight to message bank. When it did, hearing her voice was painful. He sought to veil his heightened adrenalin and the familiar inflection of aggression in his voice, "Come on Sophe, you know everything is not as simple as this…Just speak to me, I can come to where you are, we can talk about it."

He slammed the phone down sending items on the dressing table flying.

"She won't talk to me," he yelled at Jai, "I need to find her, I've gotta go…" He made for the door staggering past Jai, who grabbed him.

"You won't be able to find her, man." Dylan struggled to free himself. Jai held him.

"I will. I have to…" He pushed Jai against the wall.

"If she doesn't want to be found she won't be." Tim said.

"You have no idea what I'm going through. Stay out of it."

"She's come back," Tim said with concern.

"This time is different, she's determined," Dylan said walking out the door. Jai followed Dylan onto the street.

Dylan stood on the sidewalk of Kent Street, inner city Sydney. The din of traffic, people's voices and laughter from nearby restaurants and clubs provided a cacophony of sound, in the cool evening air. Dylan bent over and nearly threw up. Jai approached him.

"What the fuck am I going to do?" He looked up from his hunched over position.

"Don't know mate, but I'm here for you."

"I feel safe with Sophie. What if she really does leave me?" His eyes were wide and his face crooked with fear.

"I don't know Dylan, but maybe you should think about how she felt with you."

Dylan and Jai walked to a bar on George Street. Dylan rang Sophie's phone repeatedly, with no reply. After many drinks they found their way back to their hotel in Elizabeth Bay. Jai stayed with Dylan, downing more shots of vodka in his room and listened to Dylan's bleary-eyed ramblings about Sophie and their fights recently and how it couldn't be over. Eventually, Jai went to his own room to sleep.

Sitting on the end of his bed, Dylan blinked through the haze of copious amounts of scotch and vodka. He did take cocaine on occasions but not this evening. He wept lying face down on the bed. Everything seemed to be caving in on him. He felt like he couldn't breathe. He took out the picture of Sophie and Zac and Angel in his wallet and traced their faces with his fingers. Tears obscured everything before him.

Images of his mother's peaceful features, her green eyes when the essence of her life left them and she breathed her last, overwhelmed him now. His mother, his only safety was gone. Now this overwhelming grief swept over him, as if it had happened again. An insurmountable emptiness, pain and abandonment seemed to cave him from within – only this time he didn't think he could survive it.

He went to the drawer next to his bed where he kept his pills, sleeping pills mainly, though he had others for anxiety and depression as well. He examined the bottle. Opening his mouth he swallowed a large handful of the small white pills with a shot of vodka, and laid down on his bed, closing his eyes he imagined his mother in her floral dress that played in the wind, hanging washing in their backyard and smiling at him in their swimming pool. Picturing Sophie or his kids was too painful. He surrendered now; the fight was over.

***

"He's tortured, Jaz." Sophie said to Jasmine sitting in her living room late that evening.

"Do you still love him?"

"Love him? I think love became fucked up a long time ago, Jaz. I feel numb, nothing. There were times he was humble and pleaded with me and for a while he would be different, and then it would go back to how it was, switched sometimes in a moment, like a split personality. He doesn't seem to have a conscience. I've realised something though, Luke's addicted to the fame, attention, women and can't feel good about himself without it. Me? I've been addicted to him."

"Sweetheart, you'll be ok. I'm here for you." She touched Sophie's hand.

Jasmine got a call on her phone, "What? Luke? In hospital? What for?" Jasmine listened to her husband David on the phone and turned to Sophie whose face was distraught.

"He's in hospital, Sophe."

"What? What do you mean?" Sophie said, rising to her feet from the couch as if it was an involuntary action.

"He overdosed on sleeping pills."

"I can't breathe Jaz..." Jasmine took Sophie in her arms. "Is he ok?"

"He's okay, Sophe. It's not your fault."
Sophie cried into Jasmine's shoulder.

***

He opened his eyes as the scent of her perfume permeated the room—embracing him. She looked smaller, frailer in a way he couldn't define as she walked towards his bed. Like a flower separated from its source—browned at the edges and with petals precariously threatening to fall. Her shoulders seemed more exposed, the bones in her neck protruded from her green singlet, her body so familiar and beautiful, had always provided a sharp pain inside, bitter sweet like something he longed to possess mixed with dark regret, and inner unworthiness. Her hair was down, barely brushed, she had no makeup on, and her green eyes regarded him with a weariness he had not seen in her before. Darkness framed her eyes. Dylan could barely look into them they seemed to blink away tangible pain. Tears traced her cheeks.

"Oh Dylan," she said barely audible. She took his hand.

"You never call me that," Dylan said, looking down at her fingers in his.

"I'm so glad you're ok."

"Sophe."

"Are you ok?" she asked.

"I'm ok," Dylan said, forcing a smile.

"You need help."

"I know," he said.

Dylan was pale, the lines in his face looked like crevasses, deep, chasms concealing underlying truth. Apparatus was attached to his chest, small round circles with winding chords, an IV in his wrist and a machine monitoring his heartbeat displayed green lines of security. He looked at Sophie as if he was a child craving his mother.

"Please get help. Think of Ange and Zac. We can't lose you."

"I know. I'll try." He glanced into her face. She said nothing. "I know you've heard it before, sometimes we all need a wake-up call. I've always been doing my best, Sophe you know that."

She looked down and let go of his hand.

"What about us?" Dylan didn't like the sound his voice made uttering these words.

"I don't know. It's more important you think of the kids. I should let you rest. I'm so glad you're ok. I was so worried when I heard. I'll bring the kids in tomorrow, ok? They really want to see you." She kissed her hand and placed it on his. "So glad you're ok."

"Thanks Sophe. I love you."

Sophie smiled slightly, though she did not look into his eyes. Her lips formed a straight line and her gaze became vacant like seeing an abandoned house on the inside when all human inhabitants had left. Dylan had not seen this in her features before. She stood up and left, leaving only the scent of her presence. He closed his eyes—he did not want to see, anymore.

GRACE

Grace

"Don't worry, Allah is with you." The man spoke in Arabic into the bloodied ear of his son, whose eyes were frozen. He closed his son's eyes and held his hand, as they moved the gurney down the hospital aisle. A bandage covered the crimson mark on his head where the bullet had torn through his skull.

"Ahmed, He will welcome and protect you now. Forever, you will always be safe." His thick Arabic accent echoing through the corridors. His quiet weeping was heard through the corridor, his black mass of hair fell over the chest of his still, small boy.

***

Ismail had woken early that morning and after performing his Islamic prayers had gone into the kitchen and saw Ahmed eating his breakfast. Ahmed had already visited the mosque and had helped his mother make tea for everyone; he felt she didn't get enough help around the house.

"Morning, son." Ismail sat down next to him at the table.

"Morning, Dad. Have you noticed the Israeli tanks closer at the moment?"

"Yes son, but we don't have to worry."

"What can we do Dad? We can't just let them do whatever they want."

"We cannot take things into our own hands son. When you get older you will understand better. We have to trust our leaders to work it out. Killing never solves anything."

Ahmed was starting to associate with friends who were more militant about the Israeli occupation. This worried Ismail. The tanks and soldiers were encroaching closer to their part of Jenin. Ahmed had grown up in this refugee camp with its abject squalor, the dust and hardship of living in poverty.

Ismail had sought to keep Ahmed from as much of the hatred of the conflict as he could. He didn't want to indoctrinate his son. Ismail hoped these issues would be resolved by the time Ahmed was an adult.

Pretending to be freedom fighters was a favourite game of Ahmed and his friends. That was why he had pleaded with his father to buy him the replica machine gun for his birthday but his parents had refused.

"Don't worry yourself, Ahmed. Allah is in control."
"Yes, Dad."

"I'm going outside now, Dad, Ah'man is coming over soon."

"Sure." Ismail touched Ahmed on the shoulder as he got up.

Ismail had watched his son's thin petite body walk out the door. His twelve year old form disappeared into the sunlight. As Ahmed came around the corner only the top of his shining black hair could be seen. He called out to Ah'man, his friend who was playing with Jusef in the dirt with their new toy guns. Ahmed walked over and asked to borrow one of their guns. It was a replica uzi.

Standing up from the dirt he called to his friend Jusef who was running away and pretended to shoot, pointing the gun directly at him. Then a machine gun thunder assaulted the air, the sound of grinding metal, Ahmed fell sideways, as if a wall had just hit him, into the dirt. Still breathing, he could not speak only taking deep breaths in and out, his friends ran to him. Blood began to form a halo around his head in the dirt.

Ismail was sitting in his lounge room with the newspaper when he heard the terrifying bang that clattered through the air. In that moment, terror overwhelmed him. Instantly, he was at the door and yelling his son's name into the oblivious, sun-drenched day. His first thought made him feel guilty, "Please, not my son." Then he saw Ahmed's crumpled body, like those toys that collapse when you press the button, only he wasn't going to bounce up again. A toy machine gun was lying next to Ahmed's limp hand.

"No!" His father's high-pitched panic was heard across and down the street that had now fallen completely silent. Ismail ran to him screaming his name into the deaf air. He picked up Ahmed's tiny body. Blood dripped onto and mingled with the sandy dirt around him. His t-shirt was covered with the dark liquid, his eyes were afraid as he looked at his father.
"I love you, Ahmed," Ismail said as he cradled him. Ahmed looked into his father's eyes—his breath was short and sharp. Israeli soldiers had come over to investigate and the other boys held up their hands and showed the toy guns to them. The young soldier who had pulled the trigger, walked closer, stopped and collapsed onto his knees a little way off, hiding his face in his

hands. Ambulance sirens cascaded, like a strange mourning bird, wailing through the still air, as Ismail held his son in his arms and whispered to him, kissing his face, weeping and pleading with him not to die.

***

Dr Rosenthal had arrived for his usual mid-morning shift at the hospital. Noticing Ismail and his son, he walked straight over and behind the reception desk.

"Why is this man here?" Dr Rosenthal asked Miriam, the brunette nurse.

"His son was killed by a soldier and we were the best hospital to deal with this."

"Shouldn't his son be going to the morgue?"

"It says," she pointed to her clipboard, "he's going to be an organ donor."

"Really? Here, in an Israeli hospital?"

"Yes, I know it's unusual," she whispered. "His son is killed by an Israeli soldier and yet he is here donating his son's organs to us."

Dr Rosenthal was speechless. He could not stop looking at the man.

Ahmed's trolley was wheeled past the desk and into the cubicle adjacent. His body was attached to various machines that were keeping his heart pumping blood to his vital organs. Dr Rosenthal could hear Ismail—the man didn't look unlike himself; curly, dark hair, thick eye brows and light green eyes—talking to his son. Dr Rosenthal could understand Ismail as he was fluent in Arabic and had spoken the language more than most Israelis, due to his volunteer work with Arabs in Gaza.

"No one should go through this, Ahmed," he was saying. "Not even our enemies. You'll see everything clearly when you see Allah, you will be at peace." His words were barely audible as he sobbed.

Slowly and gently Dr Rosenthal pulled back the curtain, making sure the man wasn't startled.

"Hello, I'm Dr Rosenthal," he told Ismail in Arabic, "we will take good care of your son." Ismail looked at the Dr and nodded in a grateful manner.

Dr Rosenthal wanted to hide from Ismail's wide-eyed stare.

"His mother will be arriving soon from a relative's house. Can we stay with him a while?" Ismail asked.

"Of course," Dr Rosenthal said, "anything you need, let me know."

"Thank you."

Walking out of the cubicle, Dr Rosenthal felt disoriented and he didn't know why. He had seen this kind of thing all the time on the news in Israel. He had received casualties from Palestinian bombs and comforted many Israeli parents with similar losses. However, this man was different. Where did this man put his anger from losing his son at the hands of Israeli soldiers?

It was unnerving to the hardened doctor, having lived his whole life in Israel. He wanted peace with the Palestinians, but he understood it wasn't that simple, or was it? Dr Rosenthal wanted a lasting solution to the suffering he saw everyday caused by this endless conflict and he wanted the Palestinians to also have a place and a chance for a normal life. Dr Rosenthal walked quickly down the corridor to the bathroom. He looked at himself in the mirror, tears appeared in his eyes.

"What's wrong with you?" he said, to the person in the mirror, "get it together, be professional." He splashed water on his face; he had to get back to work. Something had changed inside, somehow, a question seemed to sit in the place where resignation had been. Ismail's words, his soft tone, whispering to his son played over and over rhythmically in his head. Dr Rosenthal didn't know whether this action would impact anyone or make people take notice. He hoped it would. But he did know that whatever happened, he would never forget the morning this Arab man came into his ward and showed him, a glimpse of unthinkable compassion.

***

Two days passed of shifts treating people in the emergency ward, eating dinner in his small apartment and sleeping, but Dr Rosenthal couldn't get the Arab man out of his mind. He kept seeing the little boy's face, the bandages and the gentle tone of his father.

He was on his way to the hospital when he saw *The Jerusalem Times* newspaper and bought it, as he always did. On the second page he saw him, the Arab man and his wife pictured with the title "Ahmed's gift of Life" and began to read. Tears filled his eyes as he read about how Ahmed was shot by soldiers and then this:

"The army apologised with unusual speed. The armed factions entrenched in the Jenin camp made no calls for revenge. But it was the reaction of Ahmed's parents that caught everyone off guard. The Palestinian family donated Ahmed's organs for

transplant. The boy was in an Israeli hospital and his parents understood that their son's body parts were most likely to save people routinely spoken of as "the enemy" in Jenin. Within hours, Ahmed's heart, kidneys, liver and lungs were transplanted into six Israelis, four of them Jewish

The move was hailed by stunned Israeli leaders as a "remarkable gesture for peace", particularly given the circumstances of Ahmed's death, and a bridge between warring communities. Ariel Sharon's closest cabinet ally, deputy Prime Minister Ehud Olmert, telephoned Ismail to praise his "noble gesture". The speaker of the Israeli parliament praised the Palestinian family for its "remarkable humanity."

Further down in the article, he read that Ahmed's mother, Abla had decided with Ismail about the donation. She was quoted as saying:

"We saw a lot of painful scenes in the hospital. I have seen children in deep need of organs, in deep pain. It doesn't matter who they are. We didn't specify that his organs would go to Arabs, Christians or Jews. I didn't want my son to suffer. I didn't want other children to suffer regardless of who they are," she said.

'My son was dead but at the same time maybe he could provide life to others and maybe he could reduce their pain. Of course my son was martyred and they were the criminals and they took his life away but we are the ones who could give life back to them. And maybe my son is still alive in someone else.

"It was a message from us to them, a message of peace for them. We are the ones who want peace and love..."

The bus pulled up, brakes screeching at his stop. Dr Rosenthal was broken out of his deep thought. He didn't want to stop reading the article. He was shocked and moved by the events that had unfolded, but he folded it carefully up in three places and placed it under his arm. Wiping away the tear under his eye, Dr Rosenthal could not help the wide smile that formed across his face. The woman in red next to him on her way to a job in travel looked at him with curiosity. His face reflected a calmness that made him stand out as he stepped off the bus.

Dr Rosenthal was in disbelief at the actions of these parents. He felt awe but also relief the world had taken notice, and that this act of kindness had stopped those in power, those with machine guns and even the average person. That the death of this small boy, would give life to others. Not just others, but those who were his "enemies," who had stolen his life, would benefit and actually receive life from him. This was the profound and mesmerising aspect that moved Dr Rosenthal, that for once, the death of an Arab boy would not go unnoticed by the world. He walked quickly towards the street of the hospital excited to share the article with Miriam.

This story is based on the real life story of Ahmed who lost his life in Israel/Jenin in 2005. His parents, Ismail and Abla showed an act of phenomenal love and grace.

http://www.theguardian.com/world/2005/nov/11/israel1

THE WALL

The Wall

"Hasn't he died yet?" Jay said, looking at himself in the mirror holding the telephone.

"That's not funny."

"Yes it is," he said, grinning. That was good shit, he thought, his feet shuffling on the floor with excess energy.

"No, he's not dead yet, close to it."

"You're doing a great job, sis. Wish someone would look out for me."

"I do."

"Yeah…" this conversation was getting old, "I've gotta go."

"Yeah, wouldn't want to keep you from your occupation."

"Very funny, Penny."

"Well, I think you should come and see him soon."

"No probs, anything for you," he said, magnanimously, "thanks for letting me know." He chuckled at how normal he sounded, like a respectable middle class man.

"I thought you'd want to know, the doctors have said the tumour has returned and he could die anytime."

"Okay, I get the picture." His smile died. "I'll come over tomorrow you know, things to do, men to see."

When Jay awoke his face was adhered to his brown cushion and he realised he had probably missed visiting hours at the hospital.

"Fuckin' Dad. He won't even give a shit anyway."

Jay eventually arrived at St Vincent De Paul Hospital and after explaining he wasn't a normal visitor but a son, he was directed to the 15th floor, bed 42a. As he walked in he saw his sister leaning over his father. Images of his mother flashed before him in her soft blue pastel blouse and white flowing skirt, her wavy light brown hair and sharp nose. He could hardly breathe.

His father's mouth fell open as he saw Jay for the first time in five years. His father's eyes darted all over Jay's face and body like a doctor inspecting a patient's decline. Red blotchy craters and sores infested Jay's face, his eyes were irritated and red and his long black hair knotted in rebellion around his face.

Yellow skin, sunken eyes and an enlarged pock-filled nose showed the effects of his father's liver cancer. You don't look so scary now; Jay smiled at the thought, as memories of his father's threatening features over his bed at night dissolved.

"Jay."

"Yep, tis me."

Jay embraced Penny; she raised her arms, briefly and limply, and patted his back.

"How are you, old man?" He moved nearer to the bed.

"Not great." His father didn't smile.

"I came to give you back something."

"What?"

"This rock, you gave it to me when I was ten. You said, 'you'll have to learn to be tough like this rock', I think I did you proud." He put the rock onto his father's lap. His father was shocked and awkward as he looked down at its grey jaggedness. He looked up at Jay in bewildered fear; Jay thought he looked like a dog wincing before an owner's scorn.

"Uh."

"I just wanted to thank you for it. I think it was good advice," Jay sniggered.

His father didn't say anything. Jay's fingers rested over his father's gnarly hand and he leant forward. Jay felt his father resist and pull back in an almost frightened manner. He tightened his grip. His father looked down and no longer looked into his eyes. Jay couldn't tell if he ashamed of himself or of his son? Fuckin' hypocrite, he thought.

"Well, I'm goin'," Jay said to Penny.

She nodded and said, "I'll see you out."

"Bye, Dad."

His father nodded and looked like he might say something, but didn't. Jay thought he looked relieved. As they reached the corridor, Jay said "don't know how you do it."

"Do what?"

"Look after him, after everythin'..."

"That's because you're not me."

"You're right; bet you're glad about that."

She looked down.

"Jay, I'd like to have you over for dinner, you haven't seen the kids for ages now."

Jay looked at Penny; he thought she must be feeling guilty about the fact that it had been a year since he had seen them.

"That'd be good," he said, "what night?"

"Wednesday, about 6:00, okay? Do you want me to pick you up?"

"Yeah that'd be good, usual place?"

"Yep," she said, "that was weird in there, why do you stuff like that?"

"What can I say? I'm my father's son."

Jay could see she was unimpressed.

"Come and see him again though Jay, it does mean something to him."

"Don't know 'bout that. See you Wednesday, yeah?"

"See you then, take care."

Penny disappeared back into the room. 'As usual, back at his side. Stupid alcoholic, he brought all of this onto himself,' he muttered. It would've been nice having a female to look after him beyond the age of 12, when his mother died. He could still see her leaning over him, her scent engulfing him as she kissed him goodnight.

It was Penny's choice to be like this with Dad, but Jay couldn't pretend. Maybe she was good at forgetting or maybe she had forgiven him, he didn't know, she never talked about it to him. The lift opened at ground level and Jay walked out onto the street.

***

Jay got out of Penny's black Saab housed in her immaculate garage. Penny had gone into the house before him to help John with the children. He walked through the garage to the television room and could hear splashing, laughing and water collisions from the bathroom. Penny's house was warm and clean, with its caramel yellow walls, vibrant abstract paintings, soft white carpet and large windowed rooms overlooking the shimmering expanse of Elizabeth Bay. He called out into the hallway and naked limbs came streaking out into the hall.

"Uncle Jay," Peter yelled and ran and embraced him. Jay picked him up.

Lucy came around the corner wrapped in a towel.

"Hello, Uncle Jay," she said, obviously pleased to see him, but not showing much emotion.

Penny followed her children, "I'm just getting him dressed." She took Peter and dressed him in his red and blue Elmo pyjamas and Lucy appeared in what Jay saw was a Saddle Club shirt and pants. John appeared out of his office and greeted Jay. They walked into the kitchen, with its white imitation marble bench tops and stainless steel appliances. John handed Jay a juice and they sat down to dinner. Jay looked around the table smiling through the dim candlelight (Penny's daughter loved candlelight). He loved Penny's family, especially his niece and nephew.

This dinner was so different from their childhood, he marvelled at how Penny had managed to create all of this. He looked over at her as she asked Lucy how her reading was going and he smiled feeling elated for her and a little envious. He chewed slowly and looked around the table. Peter was enjoying scooping his butter chicken into his pappadum and Lucy was talking about how she had been doing times tables at school. Jay surrendered to the children's stream of consciousness talking, and occasionally glanced over at his sister, who seemed happy to ignore him. The adults said nothing, until Jay asked;

"How's work, Penny?" He smiled at her and looked like he had just entered the world of grownups.

"Fine, busy," Penny said, looking over at him briefly before receiving a mouthful of food.

"How 'bout yours, John?" He smiled feeling pleased with himself to be participating in this normal dinner conversation.

"Good, thanks."

There was nothing more to be said and the children continued on, as if he always sat at their dinner table. Lucy did ask him however if he ever washed his hair, if he did wash it, why was it so knotty? When her hair got dirty or knotted her Mum washes it, she told him. He laughed and told her that was good advice.

Fear, silence and nausea were what Penny and Jay sat down to at the family dinner table. Jay thought it seemed as if Penny was avoiding looking at him, maybe his face contained too many memories. Since their father had deteriorated their childhood had been returning to him in colours, smells and scenes he wanted to forget.

Peter and Lucy sat on Jay's lap after dinner and said goodnight to him with delicate kisses on his cheek. Penny disappeared upstairs with them and John took an important call in his study, so Jay found himself on his own. He walked down into the sunken lounge room and allowed his body to relax into the red cushioning of the couch. Leaning his head backwards and closing his eyes, Jay experienced the familiar jarring of his past. Sounds pounded his skull like it was about to explode. He was glad he had taken that valium before he came, it would hold him over until he could score again. Right now, his body was anchored to the couch.

The red light behind his eyelids became the dull light of his home many years ago, one of those evenings he wanted to forget.

Jay, Penny and their Mum were enjoying a rare night of their father being away for dinner. They had been able to eat everything without indigestion and had started their homework in peaceful silence, when they heard him banging through the front door, knocking into walls, falling over and swearing at the top of his voice.

Adrenalin moved through his body, he felt nervous even at the sound of his Dad's deep booming voice. Jay remembered bracing himself for his father's

how he did give it to him, he bowled him out and then wondered if he would be beaten, but nothing happened. His father laughed and handed over the bat "Good work, Jay", the rarest comment he ever received from him. These occasions were like light falling in dense, damp rainforests, rare and enjoyable. He wasn't too bad, occasionally, when he wasn't…

He reached the hospital and walked briskly to his father's room. Penny looked up at him as he entered, her face lined with exhaustion and her cheeks splotchy and swollen.

"You're too late, he's gone." She started to cry.

"What?" He looked at his father's body, his mouth dropped open.
"He's dead?" Jay was winded.

"They worked on him after he arrested and then after 30 minutes, they declared he was gone."

Jay sat down next to the bed. He touched the edge of the bed clothing, as nausea overwhelmed him.

"You shit," he said to his father.
Penny got up and walked to the window, looking out onto the grounds.

"You were a fucked father and now you're gone, there won't be much to miss will there?"

"Why do you have to be such a bastard?" Penny turned to him.

"Why are you such a suck-up?"

She looked away again.

"Well, Dad, I guess this is goodbye. You were a fucked father anyway, so what will I be missing?" he started to cry, "what will I fuckin' miss? How can someone miss something they never had?"

Jay covered his face in his hands and cried bitterly. He raised his head, his throat aching and looked over at his sister. She was perched on the hospital chair near the window, her knees drawn up in a foetal position, crumpling her navy pin striped suit into soft layers of pastry folded onto itself. Penny's eyes were closed and her mouth was biting onto her hand. In this moment she was his 11 year old sister sitting crying in her bay window the day they lost their mother and after they both realized they had been left alone with him. Jay remembered holding her on that day, and many others, and comforting her. Now, this brotherly concern overcame him and he wanted to embrace her again. But she was a stranger to him now.

Against all his instincts, Jay got up and crossed the distance between them. He awkwardly attempted to put his arm around her shoulder. She jumped forward in shock and pushed his arm away. He moved back, startled.

"What are you doing?"

"I was trying to comfort you or something..."

"Well don't. You've never given a shit before, so why would you start now?"

"I thought..."

"The thing is Jay, you don't think... Not about me, anyway."

"That's not true."

"Of course it is, right now you're probably thinking of how you can get out of here and score something."

"Very amusing, Penny, why are you being such a bitch?"

"Because you're so self-centred and you've never given a shit about me, especially when you left home and me with Dad, thank God for Aunt Jenny."

"I did think about you." He could see her little features pressed against the lounge room window the day he left home, her pleading eyes watching him leave on that dark evening.

"Yeah, in between scoring, shooting up and whatever else you do."

"Where do you get off judging me?"

"I don't."

"What do you want from me?"

"Nothing. I gave up on needing you a long time ago."
Jay looked over at his father's body.

"Anyway, all that stuff shits me and it's all done now. What's the point in even talking about it? You don't get it, even now, after our fucking father is dead."

"I do get it. But what can I do about it?" He shouted at her.

"Nothing. You are like Dad, a selfish prick. And what shits me now about all of this," she was getting louder, "is that I thought when he died...I'd feel different...better, relieved or something. But I fucking don't," she directed her words towards the body on the bed. She stood up, scraping the chair loudly as she pushed it back and stood looking out the window.

"I hate him," she muttered into the glass.

Jay was marooned in the middle of the room. He had wanted Penny to open up, but he hadn't expected this.

"Do you want me to leave?" he asked.

"Whatever you want." Her voice was altered, low, like she had run out of air.

Jay looked at his sister's immaculate clothes and her aggressive stance facing the window, but he saw in her face a vulnerability he had recognised in new men who arrived at The Wall.

For a moment, she was his little sister again, arranging her dress neatly on her lap, crying softly when the noise and violence got too much in their household. He knew she was right to be angry at him, he had been a selfish bastard, but he didn't know how to tell her this.

Penny's life crystallized for him now and he saw his neglect in it. She had suffered the most; she had borne the weight of it all. 'Penny was left twice; by Mum and by me, abandoned to deal with Dad on her own,' he thought.

"For what it's worth Penny, I love you, I can't change the past, but I'm sorry for what I've done."

He spoke quietly, looking down.

She looked over at him and he saw her eyes soften towards him and then she looked away again. Jay walked over to his father's body; kissing his hand he put it onto his father's cheek.

"Bye, Dad. It's been real." He looked into his father's face half expecting and even hoping for a sarcastic remark or a snide response. He touched his hand.

"Let me know when the funeral is and maybe, sometime, you could have a junkie like me over again."

"Yeah, maybe." She didn't look at him.

He left the room, stopping only to look back at his father. Walking out of the hospital's sliding doors into the sun, he lit a cigarette and made his way back to the bus stop.

FOREIGN OBJECTS

Foreign Objects

I could see she was sipping a tin cup of chai tea; its steam rising into the air as she blew across the surface and created waves that any surfer would envy. I salivated at the sight of the tea. It was all we drank on our expedition through the foothills of the Himalayas. A sweet aromatic scent was coming from the stone tea house sitting alone on the edge of this part of the mountains looking out into a brilliant valley of yellow and green canola terraces. Sipping chai tea was heavenly for me, with its fusion of cardamon, cinnamon, cloves, fennel, bay leaves, ginger, honey, brown sugar and milk over the warmth of a wood fire.

She doesn't speak a word of English. Jade eyes like the rushing Karnali River, a silver stud reflects light from the right side of her nose. Her auburn black hair is twisted tightly into a plait and twirled into a bun on the back of her head. Vivid turquoise, purple, yellow, red and navy flowers and birds and curvaceous patterns twist all over her sari and around her body. A marone circle sits symmetrically between her eye brows signifying her righteous piety, and either that she is married or a modern Hindu woman who wears the symbol nevertheless.

From looking at her relaxed gait one can see these mountains are her home. She knows every crack, crevice and rock from here to Joktapur. She is relaxed and seems to me to look like any 20 year old enjoying the sun and not thinking about anything in particular. She flashes us a white waterfall smile. I could feel Nepal bewitching me right now. A Himalayan spell of dirt tiered mountains, jagged rock edges framed by deep blue and white above, mountain streams no longer breathing but frozen in ice beauty, monkeys chattering and following us through the dense darkness of majestic trees in forests that reminds me of Tolkien. Our guide, Prakash, chats to the girl in Nepalese. She giggles but does not make eye contact with him. We sit down on the rock cut chair. In the distance, two parkers can be seen advancing on us. A red and a navy parker, two dark beanies, two sets of hiking boots and two walking prods striding in strong, and determined motion. Prakash leans over to me and says:

"The girl told me 'they'," he points to the oncoming travelers, "are German and are how you say, "rude," rude to her family at their lodge," he whispers.

"Oh, that's no good." I say to him.

The girl nods towards me and smiles. She obviously recognizes their mannerisms and stride. As the two continue, they keep their pace up, rhythmical and rigid. When they get closer the man says, "allo," and I say, "hello" and the others nod towards him.

Winter in Nepal, icicles jut out of caves, chasms and over rocks, and freezes waterfalls; but it won't deter these people. They are going to conquer this land and are not going to slow down or alter their paths. A stubborn blindness to the magnificent Himalayas and the medieval culture around them is evident. Nothing will distract them from their course. It is as if a mental checklist is being ticked off with every squelch of their walking sticks into the ground.

As they come nearer something else becomes obvious to us, but not to them. They do not look at us as they approach, but smile impersonally, looking off at some imaginary point straight ahead. We try to look away but find ourselves drawn back, like when you see a large hairy wart on someone's face. But this was clear and rigid, sticking straight down from their noses to their top lips as direct as the path they have set for themselves, four frozen phlegm stalactites.

I suppress my laughter and so does Jasmine, my traveling companion. The Nepalese girl puts her hand over mouth. Once they disappear over the slope, the four of us roar with laughter. Our Nepalese friend laughs the loudest and continues long after we stop.

JOSEPH'S COAT

Joseph's Coat.

He watched his German Shepherd's face disappear into the greenery of the landscaped bush. His long black snout was picking up the scents of the many animals that live and walk through Central Park. Every day they walked through this section of the park, but today was different. They would jog around the pond several times and then end their exercise with some fetching; throwing the tennis ball across the green expanse always relaxed Leroy. Today, nothing would.

Leroy leant over and patted Joseph around his neck. As he leant in closer he was overwhelmed by a faint scent of her perfume on his collar and on his back. Even though it was faint, nevertheless it was there, her L'Oreal Paris, embedded in the fibres of his fur, mixed with the oil from his skin. He leant on to him too hard and overbalanced and as he did he grabbed onto the dog's black coat. The dog fell backward and Leroy found himself lying flat on the concrete.

Joseph's hot breath was on his face and he sniffed curiously at his owner. Jonie's scent surrounded him, even though it was only a hint. It was like she was standing there above him saying, "Hey Roy, what you up to?" He wished that she was.

"Damn, sorry Joseph," he said to the dog.

Joseph started to lick his face. Always forgiving, dogs can take anything, even a weird owner falling on top of them, Leroy thought.

Jonie's perfume was like she was, fresh and inviting, not overbearing. Musk traced the edges of it. He saw himself in his kitchen yesterday, garlic and onion sizzling on the stove and the shrill noise of the phone and then him dropping the receiver and falling backwards onto the wall.

Now, he inhaled his dog's coat. It held the only thing he had left. This intangible mist. It was bizarre how a person could be reduced to this, a tiny vapour being drawn into my nostrils, he thought.

He could almost get why dogs loved smell. Her scent had always been intoxicating for him. Deep and ephemeral, it was like the French toast she used to cook in their sunlit kitchen of a Sunday morning.

Now, her red round lips, her 'you're not fooling me' smile, her curious and sceptical green eyes, were all as clear as if she was in front of him, wearing his favourite green low cut shirt. He longed to see her in this shirt again, to touch her and experience her velvety olive skin.

One sunlit green spring afternoon in Central Park Leroy and Jonie had been walking Joseph and were laughing as usual, and Jonie had seen this man they often passed who lived on a particular park bench under an oak tree. She had commented many times about him wondering if he was ok, but this time she told Leroy she was going to buy him some food. She approached him and asked him to join her for a sandwich. He looked at her in bewilderment but had risen and the three of them had gone to Tony's Diner and ordered a pastrami sandwich. Joseph of course had to sit outside but was given a bowl of water to keep him happy. There was little conversation. The man's name was John. He seemed bemused, but Jonie simply and with smiling eyes asked whether he had family, he answered no, and she bought him a coffee. He sipped and looked up at her every now and then, his matted hair and his unbathed stench made people in the café look at them. They walked John back to his bench, he had a quiet smile fixed on his face now. From then on they had a friendship and would check in with him on their walks, this was Jonie – sassy, but kind and compassionate. How could he go on without her sun?

He tried to stand up, but as he did dizziness and grief enveloped him and he dry retched into the bush. How was he ever going to escape her smell? It was everywhere, in the park, in their apartment, in her books, CDs, magazines and of course her clothes, he hadn't even ventured there.

"Come on, Jo," he said to the dog and pulled him onto the path.

Joseph followed, but quickly discovered a black Labrador female to sniff and make friends with. His nose was investigating the other dog thoroughly and the female owner of the dog laughed and tossed her long blonde hair across her shoulder. Leroy managed to smile and then pulled Joseph away.

"Yes, Joseph," Leroy said to his dog as he kept looking back to the canine they were leaving behind, "I know she smelt nice, but I'm not interested in any new scents, and I don't know if I ever will be."

Eventually, Joseph forgot about the Labrador and focused on the shrubs and footpath ahead on their way home. Leroy watched Joseph's black and tan coat and knew he wouldn't be washing it for quite some time.

SARAH

Sarah

Behind her Mum she wandered deep in thought. The corridors stretched on before her as ominous as the concept of life and death. When they reached the room she paused and took a deep breath. She pushed the door in slowly and entered smiling despite herself.

The stench of urine and disinfectant greeted her and she muffled her repulsion. It was a simple room consisting of a bed, side table, monitor and television, but all Sarah could see was the prisoner on the bed.

She made her way towards the bed cautiously and sat beside him. His face was gaunt and his bones down his neck and shoulders protruded from his anaemic skin. Sarah reached down to kiss him biting her lip to hold back tears. His face contorted in an expression of fear, fear of the pain that he anticipated would result from such a gesture. In fact this contact would cause no such pain. The morphine had numbed his body so that it couldn't in fact experience any pain. His brain still sent panic messages nevertheless. Sarah at once pulled back, in shock she turned to her mother behind her and her mother shrugged her shoulders hopelessly.

Sarah returned her gaze to her Dad who had once again become composed. She was bitterly shaken and a deep shudder was cleared and suppressed for the moment. His mouth hung open and dribble traced the creases in his face, mucus began to run from his nose.

Immediately, and without reservation Sarah grabbed a tissue and after explaining her intentions to her Dad she proceeded to clean his face up. She was gentle and meticulous. She wasn't revolted or disgusted and saw it as an instrument or tool in which she could show her love for him. She couldn't stand to see him in such disgrace not able to look after himself and this small action preserved the respect he deserved.

Sarah gazed at his ravaged body destroyed by the passage of time. She neither cried nor said anything, it seemed she could stay forever. Her mother touched her on her back after what seemed only minutes, but what had in fact been an hour and signalled that they should leave.

As Sarah stood up her legs felt weak and she supported herself on the bedside table. She looked into her father's eyes and received what words could never express. His eyes began to well up and her sobs began to fall out into the open air.

She stood up fully, leant over and gently touched her lips to his forehead, she whispered, "bye Dad, I love you", the words barely audible. She could no longer meet his gaze and began to pick her way across the floor carefully as though there were obstacles in her path. When she reached the door she turned back and offered a weak smile. He uttered, "I love you too."

As the door slammed behind her and her mother, it seemed the door had just been slammed on her Dad's life. Sarah pressed up against the door, tracing the polished pine and sobbing quietly. A high pitched whine echoed through the immaculate corridors, as Sarah began to run. The noise of her shoes slamming the hard linoleum floor seemed to scream into the silence.

She reached the hospital door and flung them open into the oblivious sunny day. She sat down on the steps of the hospital, her head in her hands. After a while something caught her eye in the park across the street. It was a father and his daughter heading for the tap. They were hand in hand and the little girl looked up at her Dad with an expression of childish awe. For a while Sarah watched the proud little girl, she reminded her of someone. Once again Sarah stood up and made her way down the steps.

(First story published, in *Studio Magazine*, NSW)

POEMS

ON THE BEACH

On the Beach

I remember...
crystal cold water on Sundays
the sun-filled car driving through winding roads
to the beach,
listening to Midnight Oil with you,
our quietness and peace
lying on our towels, sleeping off Saturday night
perfection in imagery,
salt air on my tongue,
light, ephemeral mist hangs in the air,
deep blue bracing water
draws and heaves,
raises us up and places us down,
with magnetic magic and strength,
as if the ocean had hands,
ancient rocks form temples, sitting quietly next to us,
stillness inside,
air, gently plays on our bare skin,
free and cool around us
fragments, precious silver,
glittering refractions of deep reds, purples, yellows, blues
and greens,
these reflections of light
are all I have
now
But they are beautiful beyond words.

(This is a poem about beautiful memories with my
brother, who died in 2010).

I REMEMBER

I remember

I remember sunlit, green grass summers,

I remember your cackle,

I remember that wicked reflection in your eye,

I remember your witty, cheeky storytelling,

I remember your dry humour,

I remember exploring bushland with cicadas humming a wall of sound,

I remember dry warmth,

I remember surfing with you in cold Sydney currents,

I remember the deep, dark chasmed cliffs of Bilgola,

I remember falling asleep next to you in Sunday sun,

I remember telling you *I love you* every time I saw you,

I remember you saying *I love you*,

I remember being there when you passed to the other side,

I remember lying on your chest,

I remember indescribable loss,

I remember you saying, 'don't miss me, I'm going to a better place'

I remember feeling your faith was stronger than mine,

I remember celebrating your mischievous character, your spirit,

I remember feeling your presence,

I remember us reciting poetry about you on the jetty in the dark,

I remember you.

(First published in Grapeshot Magazine, Sydney, 2015).

FORCED FAREWELL

Forced Farewell

Consciousness at 6am
Did I sleep?
Goodbye is required of me today,
I move my body-to collect my oldest friend
From the airport,
I don't notice the temperate air
Or the sky, eternally clear
My legs and arms are robotic
I drive
He gets in the car.

My body feels nothing,
This mourning—
Only a poem
Expressed
Prose too limiting,
You were never constrained.

We get out at my mother's house
The white tiled floor
Echoes emptiness
My legs nearly collapse beneath me
Like a zebra push button toy
"Instruction: Puppet collapses when base is depressed"
My legs will no longer hold me,
'Can you drive?'
He holds me up
Against the tidal surge,
My legs will not carry me
To say goodbye.

BEAUTY

Beauty

Spiked lines form
moving palms against the light sky,
All the pain of life, glimpses.
If this filled us, all at once,
we would die,
Orange, squelchy petals
face the sky,
in homage to endless perfection.

Wind, invites gaiety
within the light boughs of slim tree life,
Playfully causing a captivating dance
and sings with gentleness that –
PAIN   and   BEAUTY
are   ONE.

ONE MORNING

One morning

Diagonally across the road,
Four birds,
Flutter around one of their own,
Risking their own fate,
To be near one of their family,
or mate,
They linger close to him,
His body of light grey and black
crumpled, a captive in the arms of death,
they touch him gently with their beaks,
moving closer,
Cars bank up at the lights behind them.
I am with them,
Grieving,
The cars diesel forward
breathing heavy, caustic, hot fuel breathe
onto the birds,
Who remain oblivious to anything besides…
until deep growls from the coloured beasts,
sound the alert
The birds alight in unison
In frightened flight

No time for grieving
On this black asphalt
Of progression
No pausing for them
As humans move
drive – loud, furious motion across the earth.
The birds surrender
Their 'one' to oblivion,
Did they sing songs of grief
As they alighted?
beautiful sonic melody.

The humans bluster on towards
their next engagement,
social gathering
Oblivious also of the quiet,
gentle mourning of a family.

HIMALAYA MAGIC

Himalayan Magic

The aeroplane sits on the tarmac.
A big noisy intruder,
Outside rubbish banks up against the mesh fences,
overflowing and forced onto the wire,
breathtaking poverty,
I am paralysed
everyone has disembarked
except—
my body is shocked into heaviness,
eventually, my friend gets me to rise,
leaving the airport
a surge of brown faces,
bright eyes,
call to us,
I am 19,
driving through Kathmandu,
my eyes are hungry for every
delapidated structure,
rickshaws honking, furious movement,
diesel chokes the air,
animals wander unaccompanied in the streets,
rubbish, overgrown grass,
babies bathed in backstreets.

cows healthy and vibrant

move about with privilege,

whilst thin brown boys and girls,

sell street merchandise,

of handwoven caps or handmade chess sets

their skin heavy with dirt,

their smiles other-worldly.

a man's face

appears through a wooden shutter

framed by an ancient stone house,

his smile like a white waterfall,

he comes downstairs,

to sell us humbly,

coloured hats, bags,

hours of labour,

sold for 10$

Tokens of place,

To take home to the 'other'

his face an abiding memory,

Strength, peace, hope, hardworking humility

through grime stained hands,

small female frames

appear in the doorways of kitchens

of medieval stone cottages

set precariously
into the bossom of the green
and yellow fields
of the Himalayas,

Beauty mingled with blood, dirt,
Poverty mingled with humanity,
Stillness mingled with chaos,
Nepal, mesmerising magic,
Shocked, enlivened
and transformed me.

RED

Red

At high altitudes
We approach
Oblivious of what is below,
The cloud shifts
We see
This ancient mass of redness
Soul of the country
Massive, pulsating heart
unchanged for centuries,
at the centre of this nothingness,
surrounding
flatness
meanders like the rainbow serpent
until your eye
is mesmerised by its magnificence,
circular
shapely, curvaceous,
sensual,
contours on its form
reveal the permeable nature of the rock,
altered, changed by water
over time,
grooving, carving, evidence of deep gullies

of watery cool bodies,
sliding down its back,
as if a waterslide on a summer's day.

Colours play on your surface
throughout the hours of our day,
revealing distinct
aspects of your character
morning delicate, shy pinks, dusky greys,
gentler ochres surround you,
changing into more literal burnt orange
scorched by the heat of midday,
sun unflinching above,
then you return towards rich reds,
deliciously mingling
light blue and deep blue,
vivid red and violet
bleeding into sky blackness,
You are spectacular.
You quietly perform for us,
Profound and beautiful,
Some of us climb you,
trampling over sacred ground.

Stillness in the place
of water,
sacred to Indigenous women,
air plays in the trees,
almost whispers with ancestral voices,
a corroboree with deep digeridoo sounds,
human voices of high and low calling
mingle rhythm with tribal drums,
pulsing near us,
a recording but profound,
in the vast quietness,
of no one around
still, an abiding presence in this place.

An expansive presence
one cannot look away from,
a shrine of worship,
a sacred temple,
Nature's grand cathedral.

On our journey,
I spot a camel,
Finding shade under a gum,
I stop the car,

and move towards the reclining animal,

he is chewing,

his mouth moves in slow, circular motion,

his jaw clicking,

he looks directly at me

wonders why I am walking closer to him,

I can see he considers whether to get up,

this place is slow however,

he decides against it

as I stop,

I am a spectacle to him,

with my black object

protruding from my face,

we regard one another,

two beings

sharing

this quiet moment

together.

ABOUT THE AUTHOR

Suzanne was born and grew up in Sydney, her family lived in the US when she was young. Since Suzanne was a small child she has been fascinated with words. After graduating university with a journalism and literature degree, Suzanne worked as a freelance journalist for 20 years. In this time she wrote for many different publications and most recently has graduated with a Master of Arts in Creative Writing in 2017.

Throughout her life Suzanne's writing career blossomed, in journalism, but also creatively. Her short stories and poems have appeared in many journals over the years, including in *Compassion: A Creative Anthology, The Quarry Journal, Grapeshot Magazine, Studio Magazine, Time Off and Heretical magazines.*

Her journalism has been published in many publications including; *AMG Magazine, The New Internationalist, The Sydney Morning Herald, The Big Issue, The Review Independent Monthly, Boardwalk Magazine* amongst many others.

Her book ***Freedom Writing*** has been **Number 1 Best Seller on Amazon USA** and **Australia.** Suzanne's poetry received an award from the SCLA Annual Writing Competition and her short story on Amazon Shorts came

6th out of 300 entries. Her novel, *Where the Sun Rises* was launched in October, 2019. It was Number Hot New Release in Amazon USA and Number 1 Best Seller in Amazon Australia in two categories. *Where the Sun Rises* was a semi-finalist in the Screencraft Cinematic Book Contest in 2019.

For further information about Suzanne you can visit www.suzannestrong.com or www.suzannestrong.net. You can join Suzanne's email list to receive updates on her latest releases.